Pop
and the Fat Cat

by Susan Hartley • illustrated by Anita DuFalla

Pop and the fat tan cat
can nap.

Pop is on the cot.

Is the tan cat
on top of Pop?

The cat is not on Pop.

The fat tan cat is on the cap.

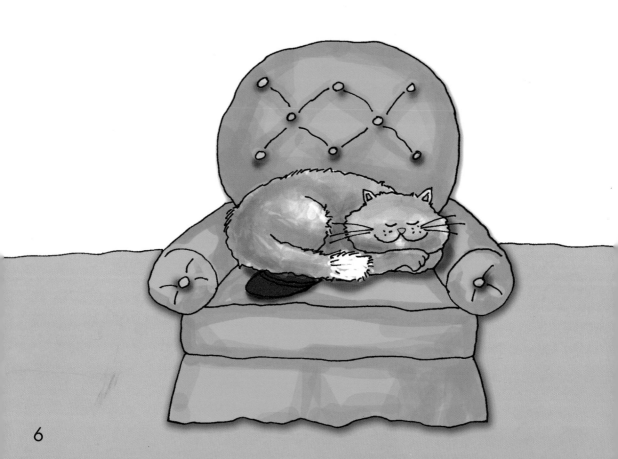

Pop is not on the cot.

The cat is not on the cap.

The cap is not fat.